Finster Frets

by
Kent Baker

•

illustrated by
H. Werner Zimmermann

Toronto   Oxford   New York
OXFORD UNIVERSITY PRESS
1992

Oxford University Press, 70 Wynford Drive, Don Mills, Ontario, M3C 1J9
Toronto   Oxford   New York   Delhi   Bombay   Calcutta   Madras   Karachi
Kuala Lumpur   Singapore   Hong Kong   Tokyo   Nairobi   Dar es Salaam
Cape Town   Melbourne   Auckland

and associated companies in
Berlin   Ibadan

Canadian Cataloguing in Publication Data

Baker, Kent, 1938–
Finster frets

ISBN 0-19-540899-3

I. Zimmermann, H. Werner (Heinz Werner), 1951–
II. Title.

PS8553.A383F5 1992   jC813'.54   C91-095649-9
PZ7.B35Fi 1992

1 2 3 4 - 5 4 3 2

Printed in Mexico

Poor old Finster awakened one morning with a bird nest in his hair.

"What's this?" he asked. "Has someone strawed my topside? Has someone broomed my brain?" For at this point he could only feel the nest with his fingers, and Finster thought his fingers might be fooling him.

"Let's have a look-see," he said, as he kicked aside the bedclothes and crick-creaked over to the mirror.

"Well tickle my toes!" he exclaimed. "Jumpin' jivin' jellyfish if I don't have a bird nest in my hair!"

And indeed, there, staring back at him from the snarly brink of that hairy nest, were four bird eyes roundly planted in two bird heads.

"What are ya doin' there, ya silly creatures?" Finster demanded. "Do I look like a tree t'ya? Do ya think I'm a bush? Get off me. Shoo!" He wiggled his fingers at them and made scare-the-birds-away faces, but the birds sat firmly in place. No matter what the old man did, they remained unperturbed.

"By thunder!" he shouted. "I need help." And he hurried down to where his wife, Holly Berry, was busy preparing fiddle-faddle pancakes and rice berries for breakfast.

"Holly Berry, my faithful, my fortress, my white-haired puppy love, look what I have on my head!"

Holly Berry turned and smiled at Finster. "You silly old salami," she laughed. "What are ya doin' with a bird nest on your head? Do ya think it's April Fool's Day or Hallowe'en, maybe? You're one funny man, all right, I grant you that." She turned back to the wood stove.

"No, no, no, my sugar cake!" he shouted. "It's not a joke. After I woke up this morning I was building up to doing my yippee yawns and stretches, when all of a sudden I felt a strange tug at my hair, and there they were. And here they are! Please, get 'em off. No one's going to take a man seriously when he's got birds nesting on his head."

Holly Berry still thought Finster might be funnin' her, having one of his jokes, but she slid the fry-pan to one side and leaned over for a closer look. "Well, I'll be!" she said, as she poked here and pulled there.

"Ouch!" Finster cried.

"Don't fret, Finster," Holly Berry said reassuringly. "Hold still. There's never yet been a knot I couldn't untie, or yarn I couldn't unravel." She twisted, pulled, picked, plucked. She dibbed, she dithered, she dabbed. She tried. And she tried. And she tried.

Finally, with a big sigh, she flopped down in her rocker. "Well, I never . . ." she said.

"I never either," he said, "until now."

"Why, that bird nest is as tight to your dome as a bung in a barrel," she said. "Right rooted it is, like hay to a hill. Tip me from a tower if it don't seem to have grown there all on its own."

Finster was getting desperate now. "Don't just stand there! Gawking doesn't gather eggs. Do something! Frighten them. Tell them we have ten hungry cats.

Tell them we just love bird pie and feather porridge. Tell them anything, just so they go away.''

Holly Berry thought hard for a minute. She did all her thinking tricks. She tugged at her ears. She rubbed her nose. She took great deep breaths into her belly.

''I got it!'' she cried. ''Hitch Wind Dancer to the wagon. We'll ride them critters away.''

So, off they went, Finster in his nightshirt and Holly Berry in her housecoat. They raced through the countryside. They sped around corners. They bounced across brooks. They pounded over trails.

"It's no use," Finster shouted. "They won't come loose. They must have lead in their tails."

So they stopped. Wind Dancer, who was completely bushed, stood resting, while Finster and Holly Berry plopped down on a sunlit rock.

"Why'd this happen to me," Finster moaned.

"Why not to you," Holly Berry said. "If it had to be someone, I mean, 'cause you must admit, you have some fine head of hair for nestin' in."

"*Had*, you mean," Finster replied. "Now I got a bird nest instead. And with unwanted tenants to boot. Hey, up there," he shouted, "if you don't leave, I'm raisin' the rent! I'll sublet my ears to a weasel. I'll set fire to my eyebrows."

The birds tweeted happily.

"I give up," Finster said. "I'll just have to be a human bird-pole until it snows — or maybe forever." The thought made Finster sad.

"Don't worry so, ya old box of socks, or I'll have ta start callin' ya Finster Frets," Holly Berry said. "Besides, we didn't live all these years and not learn a thing or two. They've got the bird brains, not us. We'll come out on top yet."

"But they're on top now," Finster said.

"Finster Frets, get up," Holly Berry ordered.

"What?"

"Get up on your pins ya old clown. You're goin' in that pond. Birds like deep water as much as seeds like crows. Go on, get in. I'll hold your night rags."

Finster Frets stripped off his nightshirt and walked deep, deep, deeper into the water . . . to his waist . . . to his chest . . . to his shoulders . . . to his chin. Suddenly he stopped.

"I don't know how to swim," he said. "I'll drown if I go any further. I'd rather be alive with a barnfull of birds on my head, than be supper for fish, crawlies and crawdads."

So, dripping wet, Finster came out of the water and he and Holly Berry rested and thought again.

"I got it!" Finster declared. "I'll climb that tree there and dive down on my head. The birds won't want to be crushed, so they'll fly away."

"Wonderful idea," said Holly Berry sarcastically. "And after you're through, I'll sweep up what remains of you. Then I'll puzzle how a soupy pile of grizzle and bone is going to keep me company next winter."

"Woe is me," Finster sighed. "I got birds in my belfry and feathers atop my tree."

"Well, no sense setting here," Holly Berry said. "Let's head home. We'll give it some more thought. Maybe an idea will steep."

When they arrived back home, they sat and sat and sat. In fact, the silence grew so silent, the birds had a nap.

Two tears moved slowly down the cracks and crevices of Finster Frets' worried face. Two more followed. He was sadder than an empty basket. He was sad from the ceiling to the floor. He was sad from China to Chile. Why, Finster Frets was sadder than the whole universe! He decided to blow his nose.

"Honk," he blew. "Honk. Honk."

The birds stirred.

"Honk. Honk."

There was a fluttering from his topside.

"Keep blowing!" Holly Berry shouted. "Blow from the soul. Blow from your toes. Blow your socks off. Blow. Blow. Blow!"

And he did. He blew, and he blew.

"Honk. **Honk.** HONK. **HONK!** *HONK!*"

And the birds flew out of the nest and up into the air. They flew from kitchen to parlour, around furniture and plants. They flew past pictures and pots, past knick-knacks and lamps with Finster's honk close behind.

"Open a window," he shouted. "Open a door. Once they're gone, they won't be here any more."

Holly Berry did just that and out they flew.

"We did it! They're gone." Finster began to jig. Holly Berry joined in.

They leaped, leaned, twisted and twirled until all of a sudden three eggs tumbled from Finster's head and fell to the floor.

"Eggs!" they both shouted, as they dropped to their knees to examine them.

"They're not broken," Finster said. Why, in fact, these aren't even eggs. They're coloured stones!"

"Well, what do you expect," Holly Berry asked, "from birds who nest in hair? I'm amazed they knew how to fly. Wouldn't have surprised me to see such mixed-up birds hopping away like bunnies or crawling away like snakes. Anyway, the main thing is, they're long gone and far from our home."

So, the old couple sat down to a late breakfast and spent what was left of the day relaxing.

That night in bed, Finster dreamed all manner of strange things, like carrots chasing rabbits and flowers eating stones. When he awoke the next morning he was about to do his yippee yawns and stretches when all of a sudden he felt something very unusual and very, very strange. It wiggled and criggled round and round between his toes.

At first Finster started to fret. He sat up soldier straight and glared nervously at the bedclothes. Then he smiled, eased back down, pulled the covers up high and carried right on stretching.

It — whatever it was — could wait. After all, a little wiggle and criggle was nothing to worry about.

As long as he had Holly Berry by his side, and such a wonderful honker to honk with, Finster would never fret again.